Farmer Jon's
VERY
SPECIAL
TEAM

ISBN 978-1-63814-102-0 (Paperback)
ISBN 978-1-63814-103-7 (Digital)

Covenant Books, Inc.
11661 Hwy 707
Murrells Inlet, SC 29576
www.covenantbooks.com

Farmer Jon's
VERY
SPECIAL
TEAM

BJ Oquist

Illustrated by Diana Sill

Jon is a farmer.

1

He loves many things about his farm. He loves growing carrots, radishes, lettuce, corn, and tomatoes in his garden.

2

Jon loves working with his tractors and machinery to mow, rake, and bale hay for his cows to eat in the winter.

4

Mostly he enjoys his dog, cats,

and especially his cows and horses.

One day, Jon talks to farmer Ed, who has many horses on his farm.

Jon sees this one horse he just *has* to buy! She is very young, less than one year old, and Jon names her Pearl. Pearl is yellow, like the sun, with a white mane and tail, a palomino.

Pearl is a Percheron. A Percheron is a breed of horse that will weigh two thousand pounds when full-grown! They were used for plowing and hauling heavy loads on farms, before farmers had tractors to do this work. Percherons are normally black or gray in color, never palomino.

As a yearling, Pearl is all knees and elbows with great *big* feet!

Pearl is mellow and calm with her head down, paying attention to Jon, and eager to please.

Jon enjoys Pearl so much that he went back to farmer Ed to buy another horse just like Pearl. He wants a matched team of horses, a team of two horses that look alike, working together to pull a wagon or plow.

Jon is lucky. Pearl's mother has just had another baby, a full sister to Pearl, who happens to be a palomino too! Jon is very excited and bought this little filly right away.

While Pearl's sister is too young to be separated from her mother, Pearl keeps growing bigger and stronger every day.

Jon wants Pearl to learn how to pull his wagon. He sends her to a farm that teaches horses how to do the work of a farm. Pearl is gone for her schooling for several weeks.

While Pearl is gone, Jon builds two tie stalls in his barn especially for Pearl and her sister. A tie stall is a place with a feedbox and a big bin for hay in the front, where you tie your horse but is left open in the back.

One day, Jon is worried about Pearl and goes to check on her. He thinks it is very interesting to see Pearl harnessed up in the middle of all these very large, grown-up horses, pulling a plow. He has never seen so many horses harnessed together before. It is very exciting to see horses doing the work that he uses tractors to do.

Soon the summer is over, and Pearl comes home. She has grown through the summer and is eighteen months old now. It is time for Jon to pick up Pearl's sister.

Seeing Pearl's sister is much like seeing young Pearl all over again. She is yellow with a white mane and tail, all knees and elbows with great *big* feet!

But her personality is very different. Pearl's sister always has her head up looking around while prancing all over. Jon cannot decide on a name for this new filly. He thinks and thinks.

One day, while leading her around his farm yard, he thinks about how graceful she is while prancing around, so full of life-graceful like a boat, like a schooner! Schooner will be her name!

Jon continues to work Pearl with the older, larger horses that he has.

"Practice makes perfect," Jon says.

Pearl continues to gain experience and continues to learn what is expected of her as part of a team, working on a farm.

It is normal for Pearl and Schooner to spend their days in the pasture eating grass.

At night, Jon puts them in their tie stalls so they can eat oats and hay. It takes a lot of oats to make a young horse big and strong.

One summer day, it is chore time on the farm. Jon places oats in the feeders of the tie stalls for Pearl and Schooner. When he calls them, they come running into the tie stalls for their oats. Horses love oats!

Jon hasn't gotten them tied up yet when he hears this terrible racket! It is coming from the bright blue sky. He looks up, and there is an old yellow double-winged propeller airplane flying very low, overhead.

Then, he hears a commotion in the barn! *Clippity clop, clippity clop!*

In a hurry, out of the barn comes Schooner with her head shaking and her mane flying everywhere! She stops and throws her nose up into the air, pointing at the yellow airplane.

Then she shakes her head again, looks right at Jon as if to say, "Fix that, will you?"

She puts her nose down, almost to the ground, and turns and *clippity clops* back into the barn to eat her oats.

When Jon gets into the barn to tie the sisters up, Pearl is calmly eating her oats. Schooner, breathing hard, is doing her best to enjoy her meal after it was interrupted by that loud noise.

SCHOONER

PEARL

A year later, when Schooner is old enough, Jon uses Pearl to train Schooner.

After Schooner is trained, he loves to hook them up to his dark-green wooden wheeled wagon with the red seat on top.

Two palomino sisters, with their black harnesses, pulling Jon's fancy green wagon in the small town parades, close to his farm.

Pearl so steady and calm. Schooner always prancing. They look very dapper with their white manes and tails flying.

No one else has a team like this one. This team is very special!

ABOUT THE AUTHOR

BJ Oquist grew up on 120 acres in Missouri. This acreage was truly a family farm, complete with a garden, pets, and the farm animals. As an adult, BJ worked for the state of Minnesota for twenty-six years. After retirement, BJ and her husband moved to New Mexico and are enjoying all the sunshine that the southwest is known for. Between BJ and her husband, they have five children and eleven grandchildren.

ABOUT THE ILLUSTRATOR

Diana Sill is an artist/illustrator, with a studio in Isle, MN. She has been an artist for decades, winning awards in state and county levels at art shows, as well as doing public caricature events and teaching painting classes. One of Ms. Sill's pieces is on permanent display through a Regional Art Council local to her area.